DRAGONS OF
AUTUMN TWILIGHT

DragonLance CHRONICLES

Story by **Margaret Weis & Tracy Hickman**
Adaptation by **Andrew Dabb**
Pencils by **Steve Kurth & Stefano Raffaele**
Colors by **Djoko Santiko of Imaginary Friends Studios**
Letters by **Steve Seeley & Brian J. Crowley**
Edited by **Mark Powers**

CHAPTER I

COVER BY STEVE KURTH AND BLOND

Josh Blaylock
PRESIDENT

Sam Wells
ASSISTANT PUBLISHER

Susan Bishop
VP MARKETING

Michael O'Sullivan
SENIOR EDITOR

Crank!
COMPUTER OPERATIONS

Tim Seeley
STAFF ARTIST

Evan Sult
ART DIRECTOR

Sean Dove
GRAPHIC DESIGNER

Brian J. Crowley
STAFF LETTERER

Caitlin McKay
WEBSTORE MANAGER

Kunoichi Ad Sales
773-321-8478

Licensed by:

Hasbro Properties Group

DDP

WIZARDS OF THE COAST

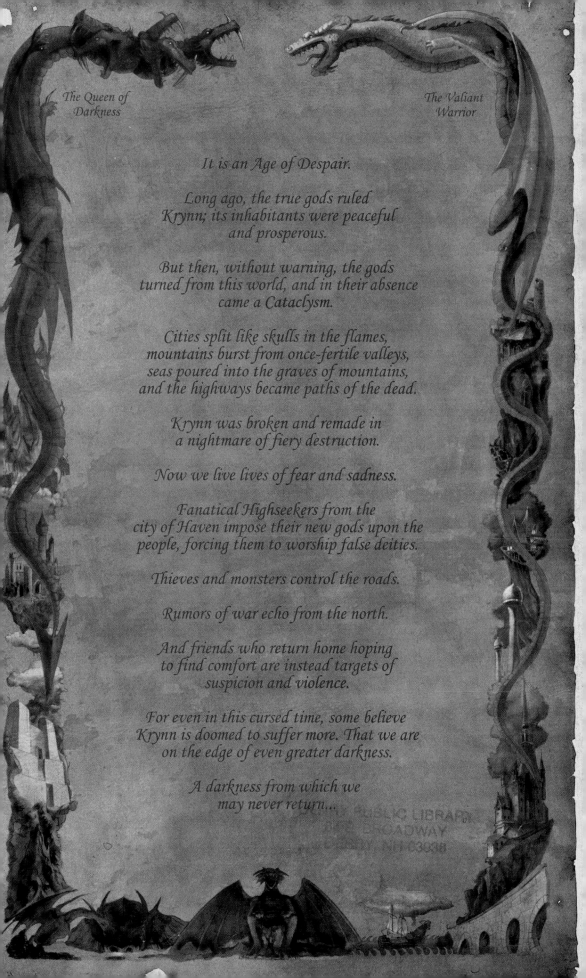

The Queen of
Darkness

The Valiant
Warrior

It is an Age of Despair.

Long ago, the true gods ruled
Krynn; its inhabitants were peaceful
and prosperous.

But then, without warning, the gods
turned from this world, and in their absence
came a Cataclysm.

Cities split like skulls in the flames,
mountains burst from once-fertile valleys,
seas poured into the graves of mountains,
and the highways became paths of the dead.

Krynn was broken and remade in
a nightmare of fiery destruction.

Now we live lives of fear and sadness.

Fanatical Highseekers from the
city of Haven impose their new gods upon the
people, forcing them to worship false deities.

Thieves and monsters control the roads.

Rumors of war echo from the north.

And friends who return home hoping
to find comfort are instead targets of
suspicion and violence.

For even in this cursed time, some believe
Krynn is doomed to suffer more. That we are
on the edge of even greater darkness.

A darkness from which we
may never return...

The Inn of the Last Home was built high in the branches of a mighty vallenwood tree, as was every other building in *Solace.*

The townspeople had decided to take to the trees during the terror and chaos following the *Cataclysm.*

And thus Solace became a tree town, one of the few truly beautiful wonders left on *Krynn.*

'TIS GETTING WORSE. PEOPLE *DISAPPEARING,* BEING DRUG OFF TO WHO KNOWS WHERE.

I'VE HEARD SOME TOWNSPEOPLE WON'T SO MUCH AS LEAVE THEIR HOUSES ANYMORE, NOT WITH THE *SEEKERS* ABOUT. THOSE FILTHY SONS OF--

ENOUGH, *OTIK!* IF THEY HEAR YOU...

PAH! UNLESS HIGH THEOCRAT HEDERICK CAN FLY, HE WON'T BE LISTENIN' TO US, *TIKA.*

YOU SEE, BOYS, WHAT *F-FOOLS* WE'RE DEALING WITH HERE IN *S-SOLACE?*

I AM *F-FEWMASTER TOEDE,* LEADER OF THE FORCES THAT ARE KEEPING SOLACE P-PROTECTED FROM UNDESIRABLE ELEMENTS.

YOU HAVE N-NO RIGHT TO BE WALKING IN THE CITY LIMIT AFTER DARK. Y-YOU'RE *UNDER ARREST!*

BRING ME THE *B-BLUE CRYSTAL* STAFF, IF YOU FIND IT ON THEM.

IF THEY RESIST, *K-KILL THEM.*

GOBLINS! IN SOLACE! THIS NEW THEOCRAT HAS *MUCH* TO ANSWER FOR!

CHAPTER II

THEN, JUST A WEEK AGO, HE RETURNED.

RIVERWIND WAS *HALF-DEAD*, AND OUT OF HIS MIND WITH A RAGING FEVER. BUT HE CARRIED THIS *STAFF*—THE ONE HE CLAIMED HAD BEEN TOUCHED BY THE *GODS*.

HE RAVED IN HIS FEVER ABOUT A DARK PLACE, A *BROKEN CITY* WHERE DEATH HAS BLACK WINGS, AND A *WOMAN* DRESSED IN BLUE LIGHT WHO GAVE HIM THE STAFF.

TWO DAYS AGO, RIVERWIND'S FEVER BROKE AND HE PRESENTED THE STAFF TO MY FATHER WHO COMMANDED IT TO DO SOMETHING, ANYTHING.

BUT *NOTHING* HAPPENED.

RIVERWIND WAS PROCLAIMED A *FRAUD* AND THE PEOPLE—MY PEOPLE—BEGAN TO *STONE* HIM.

YET MY *HEART* STILL BELONGED TO RIVERWIND, AND I DECIDED THAT IF HE WAS TO *DIE*, I WOULD CHOSE TO DIE *WITH HIM*. EVEN IF IT MEANT *FORSAKING* MY FATHER AND MY TRIBE.

THE ROCKS STRUCK US AND THEN THERE WAS A BLINDING *FLASH OF LIGHT*—

WHEN RIVERWIND AND I COULD SEE AGAIN, WE WERE STANDING ON THE ROAD OUTSIDE *SOLACE*.

THEN WE MET YOUR FRIEND STURM, AND NOW HERE WE ARE.

THAT IS THE STORY OF THE STAFF.

THAT IS *OUR* STORY.

CHAPTER III

Goldmoon laid her father rest alongside the burned and roken bodies of his subjects...

...then joined Riverwind in singing the traditional *mourning songs* of their people; high, lilting melodies tinged with sadness, regret, and pain.

HOW PRECIOUS THIS STAFF HAS BECOME,

NOW THAT IT HAS BEEN PURCHASED WITH THE *BLOOD* OF INNOCENTS.

WHAT GOOD ARE ITS *HEALING POWERS* WHEN THE MEN AND WOMEN I GREW UP WITH--THE CHILDREN I WATCHED PLAY--ARE ALL *DEAD?* WHY WERE *WE* SPARED THIS HORRIBLE FATE?

IT IS MY FAULT.

IT'S NO ONE'S FAULT, *RIVERWIND.*

WE CAN'T UNDERSTAND. WE'VE JUST GOT TO KEEP GOING AND HOPE WE FIND ANSWERS IN *XAK TSAROTH--*

YOU ARE RIGHT, *TANIS.* MY *FATHER* WOULD BE ASHAMED OF ME.

I MUST REMEMBER THAT I AM CHIEFTAIN'S DAUGHTER.

NO, GOLDMOON, NOW YOU *ARE* CHIEFTAIN.

The Draconian camp filled a huge clearing in the swamp, stretching out as far as the eye could see.

And as the lizard men moved past them, laughing and calling out insults in their guttural language, the companions were left to wonder just how large this evil army really was?

UHHH...

THEY POISONED HIM!

RAIST'S HEALTH WAS ALREADY BAD, GOLDMOON! HE WON'T SURVIVE LONG!

WE NEED TO GET YOUR STAFF BACK!

I KNOW CARAMON, I KNOW.

THERE'S SOMETHING STRANGE ABOUT THAT CREATURE.

LIKE THERE HAVEN'T BEEN DRAGONS ON KRYNN SINCE THE CATACLYSM, STURM?

NO, LOOK AT IT--IT'S NOT MOVING, NOT REACTING.

STRANGE.

Smoke from the burning Draconian camp hung over the black swamplands, *shielding the companions from the eyes of the strange, evil creatures.*

In time, Riverwind led them out of the bog and into a land cracked and scarred by the *ravages* of the Cataclysm.

WAIT!

THERE IS *WRITING* ON THIS STONE, ANCIENT RUNES OF SOME SORT.

WHAT DOES IT SAY, RAISTLIN?

"WELCOME, TRAVELER..."

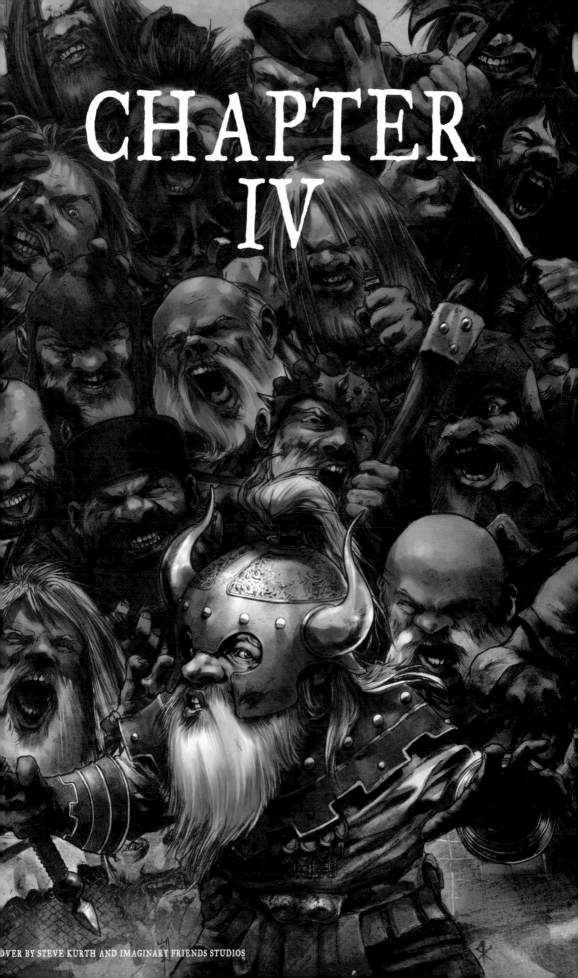

CHAPTER IV

YOU'RE ASKING A LOT OF US, *GOLDMOON.* OUR PATHS CROSSED BY CHANCE. WE TOOK IN YOU AND RIVERWIND, PROTECTED YOU.

NOW, YOU'RE ASKING ME TO ACCEPT THAT IT'S THE WILL OF THE GODS THAT *WE* SAVE THE WORLD.

AFTER ALL YOU'VE SEEN, HOW CAN YOU DOUBT, *TANIS?* YOU AND YOUR FRIENDS WANTED TO FIND EVIDENCE THAT THE ANCIENT GODS STILL EXIST. WELL, YOU'VE *FOUND* IT.

NOW, WE MUST SECURE THE *DISKS OF MISHAKAL*— WHICH WILL ALLOW ME TO CALL UPON THE POWER OF THOSE GODS.

AND THE DISKS ARE BEING HELD AT THE BOTTOM OF THESE RUINS, IN THE LAIR OF A *BLACK DRAGON*—

KHISANTH IS HER TRUE NAME, THOUGH MEN HAVE ALWAYS CALLED HER SIMPLY *ONYX.*

WHICH YOU KNOW BECAUSE YOUR *DEAD MOTHER* APPEARED TO YOU IN SOME SORT OF VISION?

AT THE BEHEST OF THE *GODDESS MISHAKAL.*

RIGHT.

YOU DO NOT BELIEVE THE CHIEFTAIN'S DAUGHTER?

NO, *I DO, RIVERWIND.* IT'S JUST—IT'S A LOT TO TAKE IN.

AND THE IDEA OF CONFRONTING THAT DRAGON, AFTER WHAT IT DID TO YOU...

BUT RIVERWIND SURVIVED, THANKS TO THE BLUE CRYSTAL STAFF THAT INITIATED THIS QUEST.

HAVE FAITH, *TANIS HALF-ELVEN.*

WHAT ARE YOU DRINKING, *RAISTLIN?*

AN *HERBAL MIXTURE, TASSLEHOFF,* IT HELPS EASE MY COUGH.

IT DOESN'T SMELL VERY GOOD. HOW DOES IT TASTE?

WORSE.

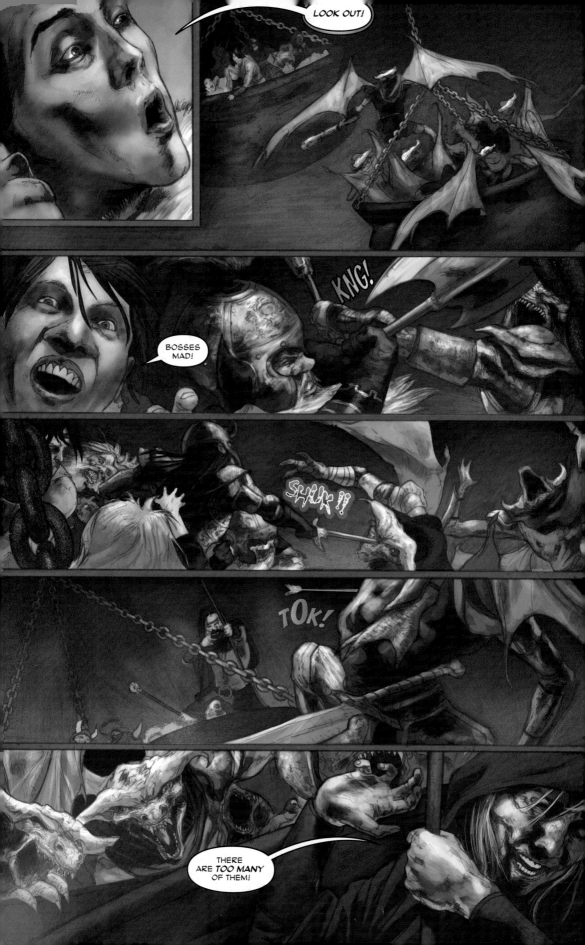

Many hours later...

BOW DOWN BEFORE *HIGHBULP PHUDGE I, THE GREAT!*

YOU HERE TO *KILL* DRAGON?

NO, WE'RE NOT.

CAN YOU *BELIEVE* THIS PLACE?

DON'T BE TAKEN IN BY THIS FOOLISHNESS. THESE CREATURES CAN BE *TREACHEROUS.*

CHAPTER V

COVER BY STEVE KURTH AND IMAGINARY FRIENDS STUDIOS

THERE! WE'LL TAKE COVER IN THE *TEMPLE OF MISHAKAL!*

TRUSTIN' IN THE GODS AGAIN, HUH?

RIVERWIND, ARE YOU--?

I WILL MAKE IT, KNIGHT.

GOLDMOON GAVE HER LIFE SO THAT WE MIGHT SURVIVE, I SHALL NOT FAIL HER!

WHAT'S *TAKING* YOU SO LONG? DON'T YOU WANT TO--

WOW...

The companions fled Xak Tsaroth, traveling toward the nearby mountains.

They saw no Draconians and supposed that those who escaped the crumbling city had traveled north to join up with the army rumored to be massing there.

It was not a heartening thought.

WHAT IS IT, LITTLE ONE?

I NEED LEAVE, NEED GO BACK TO MY PEOPLE. BUT SAD.

YOU HAVE BEEN A GOOD FRIEND TO ME, BUT AND I AM THANKFUL FOR ALL THE HELP YOU HAVE GIV US, BUT YOU MUST GO.

THE ROADS I TRAVEL ARE DARK AND DANGEROUS. I WO NOT ASK YOU TO COM EVEN IF I COULD.

YOU BE UNHAPPY WITHOUT ME.

I WILL BE HAPPY KNOWING YOU ARE SAFE.

THEN I GO, BUT FIRST YOU TAKE GIFT.

The attack had come without warning.

Even when refugees began to trickle into town—telling horror stories of huge winged monsters and a powerful warlord calling himself **Lord Verminaard—Hederick, the High Theocrat,** assured the people of Solace they would be spared.

Then came the night of the dragons.

It was over in minutes. The warriors who had pledged to protect Solace could do nothing as the dragons dove again and again, destroying everything in their paths.

And thus did Solace, one of the few truly beautiful wonders left on Krynn, burn.

That was a week ago, and much has changed.

Three buildings were left standing after the dragons' attack:

The general store, to be looted for supplies.

Theros Ironfeld's blacksmith shop, now under the control of Lord Verminaard.

And the Inn of the Last Home, because Draconians had a thirst for strong drink.

So as the endless columns of monstrous soldiers marched into Solace from the north...

...its residents were left to sift through the remains of their shattered lives, in the face of a conquering army that had gone from dark rumor to horrible reality.

WELCOME, **STRANGERS.**

MORE REFUGEE SSSCUM.

WHAT? WE'RE NOT--

SSH!

OH, CARAMON! I KNEW YOU'D COME BACK FOR ME!

TAKE ME WITH YOU, PLEASE!

YES--ER-- I MEAN... I DON'T...

CALM DOWN, TIKA, WE HAVE AN AUDIENCE.

BUT YOU DON'T KNOW WHAT IT'S BEEN LIKE SINCE THEY CAME, TANIS.

EVERY WEEK THE SLAVE CARAVANS LEAVE FOR PAX THARKAS, EXCEPT NOW THEY'VE TAKEN ALMOST EVERYONE--

LEAVING ONLY THE SKILLED LIKE **THEROS IRONFELD** BEHIND. AND EVEN **HE** ISN'T SAFE.

GUARDS! GUARDS!

GUARDS!

TING

HELP THEM!
USE YOUR *MAGIC!*

PLEASE,
IT'S *HOPELESS.*
I WON'T WASTE
MY STRENGTH.

CHAPTER VI

The survivors marched all day, following Gilthanas and his elven soldiers through the unforgiving forest...

...yet even though they were exhausted, that first sight of Qualinost, ancient and glorious, took their breath away.

THIS IS WHERE YOU GREW UP, **TANIS?!**

YES, **TASSLEHOFF.**

WOW.

THEN I'M GOIN' *TOO!* WE ALL ARE!

..., GOLDMOON ... RIVERWIND ...LD STAY WITH ...LVES AND KEEP ...E *DISKS OF* ...HAKAL SAFE, ... IT'S TOO ...NGEROUS--

I WILL NOT *HIDE* WHILE OTHERS FIGHT FOR ME!

PEACE, *RIVERWIND.*

BUT HE'S RIGHT, TANIS, WE *WON'T* STAY BEHIND.

FINE, BUT *FIZBAN AND TIKA* MUST, THEY AREN'T WARRIORS.

HA! THE GREAT FIZBAN GOES WHERE HE CHOOSES! AND I *CHOOSE* TO GO WITH YOU, HALF-ELF!

AND I'M NOT STAYING *ALONE!* BESIDES, I PLAN TO BECOME A *SWORDSWOMAN!*

SIGH

THEN IT'S DECIDED, WE'LL *ALL* GO.

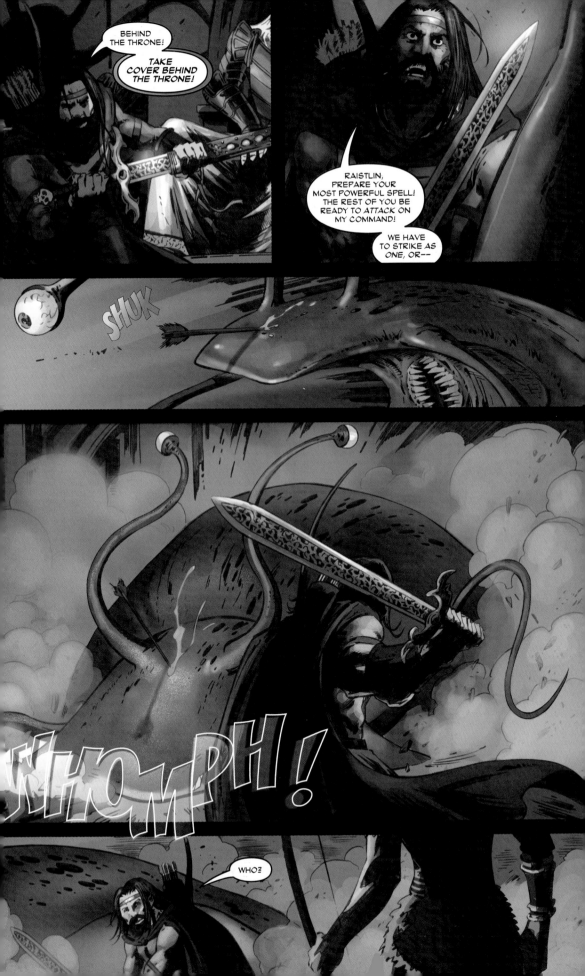

"...WELCOME TO *PAX THARKAS.*"

CHAPTER VII

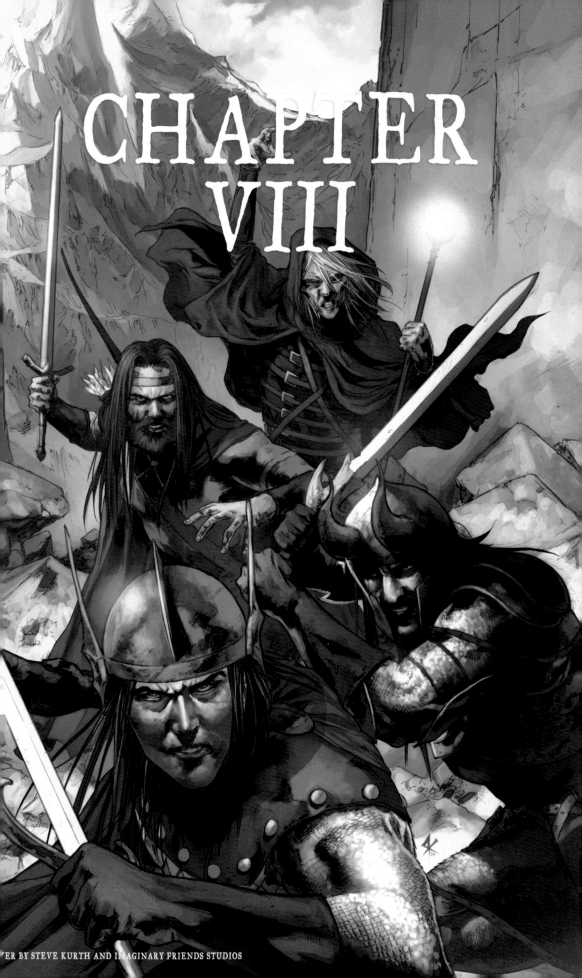

CHAPTER VIII

ER BY STEVE KURTH AND IMAGINARY FRIENDS STUDIOS

Outside the fortress.

FASTER, EVERMAN--

--I'VE BEEN PROMISED A GREAT *REWARD* FOR DELIVERING YOU TO MY MASTER.

GILTHANAS, IS THAT--?

EBEN!

TRAITOR!

WHD

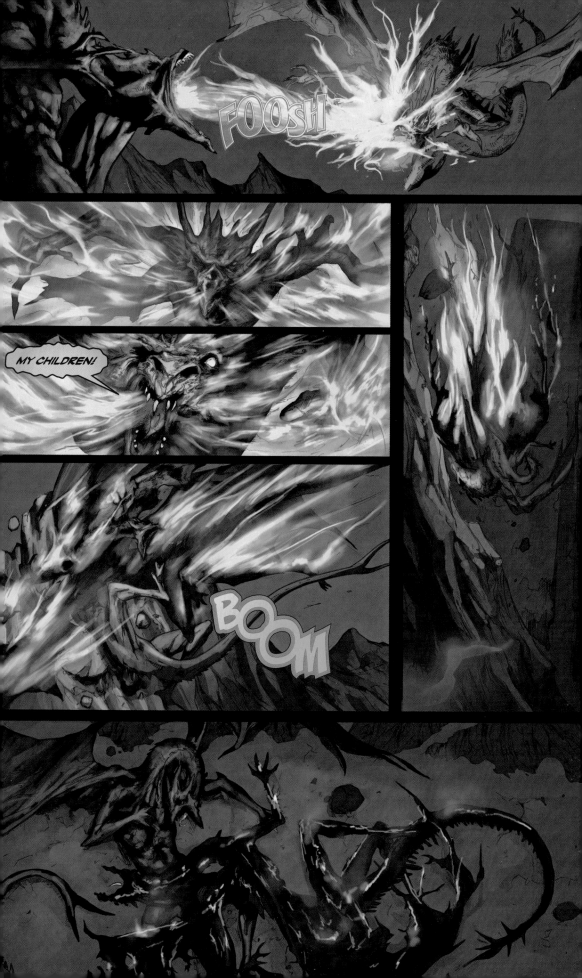

The last day of autumn dawned clear and bright as the companions led the freed slaves *away* from Pax Tharkas.

Flint, who knew these mountains well, set a course for a *sheltered valley*; one that would protect them from the coming harsh winter snows.

There the people made camp, mourned their dead, rejoiced in their deliverance...

...and celebrated a *wedding*.

RIVERWIND AND GOLDMOON.

IT WAS YOUR LOVE AND YOUR *FAITH* IN EACH OTHER THAT BROUGHT *HOPE* TO THE WORLD.

EACH OF YOU WAS WILLING TO *SACRIFICE* YOUR LIFE FOR THIS PROMISE OF HOPE; EACH HAS SAVED THE LIFE OF THE OTHER.

THERE ARE DARK TIMES AHEAD, THAT IS SURE, BUT YOUR *LOVE* WILL BE AS A TORCH TO LIGHT THE WAY.